SAY NO

SAY NO

GRACIE MOSKO

CONTENTS

Dedication vii

One	One	1
Two	Two	5
Three	Three	9
Four	Four	13
Five	Five	15
Six	Six	17
Seven	Seven	19
Eight	Eight	21
Nine	Nine	23
Ten	Ten	25
Eleven	Eleven	27
Twelve	Twelve	29
Thirteen	Thirteen	31
Fourteen	Fourteen	33

Copyright © 2025 by Gracie Mosko
All rights reserved. No part of this book may be reproduced in any manner whatsoever without written permission except in the case of brief quotations embodied in critical articles and reviews.
First Printing, 2025

To all the people who need a stepping stone.
Your trauma does not define you

CHAPTER ONE

Living as a human has its perks and it also has its downsides. A lot of people will tell you they wish they could go back in town and rewind the actions of themselves in the past. They would tell you, "Honey, you are going to do great things with your life, but do not focus too much on the future or else your life will move too fast. Do not miss being this young. You cannot get this back." You also have the people who live with the biggest regrets a person could have. Like how they served jailtime for a stupid crime that they should have not participated in, or how they decided they were going to marry their first love even though it was the most toxic relationship a person could have, or how a parent could disown a kid just for having an opinion about who is right in this world or who they should be.

This leads to many consequences you cannot reverse or change. My biggest regret is something that I can never undo, something I will live with for the rest of my life that has had so much effect on me. If someone you love does something wrong, you have a tough time hating them. You question if your judgement is off, if it is all in your head. That is what they want you to think. That is how the darkness seeps in. They commit a sin and convince you it is all ok if you do not say anything.

This is especially true if the person doing the wrong is someone you look up to with every ounce of your being, someone who listens to your problems and offers you advice on anything you need regardless of the time of day. They are there for you 24/7 because you think that they love you. You think that they have nothing better to do when in reality, they are just using you for their own benefit, so that they can please themselves and say they won the lottery. They kill you off slowly like you are a beautiful tree who is losing its leaves and then your roots get cut off. I feel like that every day, and I blame myself. I should have said no.

It was 5am and The Lady was still asleep. She had just gone to bed and probably was not going to wake up until dinnertime. It was the same thing every day and the only time you would see her was in the middle of the night when she was smashing dishes everywhere or when she would walk to the bathroom and proceed to scream at her husband for not answering her when she wanted him to. It was a depressing scene, but I found myself at their house every week for sleepovers. It did not occur to me that I was getting a little old to be sleeping over at their house, but I enjoyed the company of Him and the quiet peace in the backyard, even the minutes after what happens in that backyard. I knew what was going to happen that night, and I never did anything about it. Every day It progressed into more confusion, more questions, and more anger. Three words I forever remember, DON'T TELL ANYONE. What would I do? What could I do? Could I confront Him? Would that not break apart everything I felt I had in my life? Who would they believe? Me, the little 13-year-old girl, or Him, the one who has lived for over 50 years. I would later come to find out I thought wrong, but my life would be completely altered.

It seems so silly to say now that I loved it there because of the quiet, the games, the gameshow nights and the giggles we shared, which I truly thought were genuine. Every night I called Him, and we talked for over an hour. I do not know how I had an hour worth of conversations to talk about, but I made it fit in that time. He never talked over me and always let me cry or laugh about things before speaking or asking what I needed. He laughed with me and told me about what he did that day even if it was the same thing every day. I would wait for his calls on my birthday every year because I know he would call me and wish me a happy birthday and ask if my day was good so far. The fascination in his voice did not seem like a big deal until I got older and realized the intentions. He never actually cared; however, I did not want that to disappear because it was familiar, and I hated the unfamiliar. It brought fear to me that if I lost the familiar, it would never come back, and I would not find it again. That is never the case for anything unless you die. A part of me died that day.

CHAPTER TWO

I shut my history notebook and sighed. I will never understand why our founding fathers were important or why we need so many branches in the government. I liked science even if there were not a lot of people who shared the same fascination as I did. One time in 7th grade I learned that an adult has 206 bones and that a child has more than that. I thought that was the coolest thing in the world and I wanted to tell people. Being homeschooled it was difficult to talk to other people about what you learned, especially if all you saw in a day was your siblings and parents and those parents were the teachers. They already knew about it and my siblings thought I was crazy for thinking it was cool. The only person in my family who really showed any interest was Him. He always thought my facts were cool and He always asked questions about it to learn more. He never said I was stupid or weird for wanting to learn more about science stuff. He encouraged it, maybe a bit too much.

My sister comes in my room and asks me if I wanted to play a game of UNO and I turned it down, declaring I indeed hate UNO. My brother asks me If I want to see a magic trick. I do not, and I think that magic is silly. I do grab an encyclopedia and sit outside under the big oak tree and flip to the section on plant leaves and their processes. I want to learn more about it. I saw a page on a caterpillar, and I thought it was pretty, so I run inside and ask my mom if anyone is using the phone. She says no and that I am free to use it. I wrap my fingers around the cordless phone we had sitting in our brown cabinet and run back outside.

I am so happy; I dial all 10 digits to reach Him. He answered with a cheery "Hello honey!", my interest is now piqued even more. I start gabbing about my science book and what I learned about the bones, then adding on about the leaves and the caterpillars I read about in my encyclopedia, "and you have 206 of them bones! Is that not the most amazing thing ever? Baby Tommy has more than that but that is because he needs more protection because he is small. But you, you still have a lot. I also saw that caterpillars can be poisonous based on the color pattern of their skin. Do not touch the white and black striped ones. They are dangerous and I care about you." This conversation lasted about an hour and a half, when I looked at the minutes on the phone and gasped, telling Him I must go because dinner was ready and we were having lasagna, which is my favorite. I say bye to Him, and I hang up the phone, forgetting to respond to the I LOVE YOU BEAUTIFUL message he said. I did not catch the odd endearment in His voice.

Dinner was the same as always, Mom asks Dad how work was, Dad says it was good and almost hit a deer on his way home from work. Mom yells at Baby Tommy for throwing his peas and mashed potatoes when WE DO NOT THROW FOOD, WE EAT IT. I watched my older siblings play on their phones as they talk about how they level up on their latest game obsession, something they get into every other week but are somehow incredibly skilled at it. I see my little sister leave her food on her plate and go back to the living room to watch The Wiggles. It is more exciting than the dinner table. Was anyone going to ask me about my day? I learned something really cool. We all have 206 bones and babies have more due to the extra need for protection. No? No one is going to ask? That is ok, it is not like I need anyone to ask how my day was, I am just here.

Later that night I decided to call Him again. I was feeling sad, and I need to hear his voice, and tell him about dinner. Three rings are what I heard before He answered, "Hello honey." I tell him I can only chat for about 30 minutes because I am going to make some crafts and then go to sleep. I tell him all about dinner and how I felt alone. He never interrupted me once and I felt like I could talk for hours, but I could not tonight. I did have a brilliant idea, however. "Can I come over on Friday to have a sleepover?" He answered by asking me what I was wearing and that kind of took me off guard, but I told him my tank top and pink shorts. He answered with a cool tone in His voice and something inside of my heart shifted. He went ahead to tell me yes that I could come over and that we could go fishing while I was there. I was to be ready at 3pm. I only told my mom about the sleepover part of the phone call.

I had not realized it was Saturday night until Mom yelled down the stairs and asked me if I was going to take a shower before midnight. She wanted the water to be warm for when she got in, and wanted to be sure everyone was decent for Sunday church tomorrow. I never understood why we needed to look our best and smell our best, but she said it was so people did not think we were raised in a barn. I have definitely been around people there who smelled worse than Baby Tommy so I do not think they would care if I forgot to take a shower the previous night. I took one anyway. I sat on the floor of the tub, staring at the linoleum tiles on the shower wall. I saw the water wash away the dirt from the bottom of my feet, watching as it flowed down into the drain. That was the start of my first breakdown, and my first lie. It was fitting because the tears blended in with the water so there was no proof I was hurting. No one needed to know I was crying because they have enough to deal with. Mom did know though and I was asked what was wrong and why I was crying. I just shrugged and said I was completely fine, and they were hearing things. I know she was trying to help, and I knew she could sense when her daughter was upset but I was afraid of telling her and giving her more on her plate. I thought about it for hours until I finally fell asleep at 3am

My dreams were filled with the same old things; bad weather, anxiety, family issues, death. I tossed and turned all night and woke up at 6am sweating profusely. My heart was pounding, and I started bawling, hugging my knees to my chest. I hate these dreams, and I never understood why I was the one who had to get them. No matter what I did, they were the demons waiting for me to close my eyes and dream. Most people talk about dreams being something you hope for in the future, but my dreams are ones that want to kill me slowly. That is another branch of me that is broken. No happiness while I am awake and no happiness while I was sleeping. It was not fair, but once again, I have no one to tell this to except Him. I want to see Him now, but I still had a whole week to wait for Him.

During church we talked about how Jesus was betrayed by Judas Iscariot. I thought it was an interesting story, especially how Jesus still chose to forgive Judas even if Judas denied Jesus. I was sure to do the same if it came to it. I wanted to be like Jesus and forgiving. I felt that no one should hold a grudge against another person. You could avoid the person and situation, but forgiveness was always an option. I know I would feel so upset if someone chose to hate me forever.

CHAPTER THREE

The week went by quick for me and it is now Friday morning. I have my bags packed, one for clothes and toiletries, one for my makeup, and one for my schoolbooks. I am waiting at the window to see His grey pickup truck pull up, so anxious to get out of here and get some time away from everything. My siblings ask me when I will be back, and I tell them I will be back on Sunday because He is bringing me to church. I see His truck pull up to our driveway and He gets out. I recognize the Levi's jeans, the horse buckle belt, the cowboy hat, and the overalls He always wear and a smile creeps on my face. I am so happy I finally get to see Him again.

As always, The Lady was with him, but She did not seem happy to be here. They invite themselves inside and She chooses a spot on our couch to sit while He comes in to speak with Mom. They speak about adult things like politics and the weather, and I am bouncing around with excitement to just get out of there. I throw my bags in the back of his pickup, and I go inside to ask if we were going to leave soon. Everyone notices my anxiousness and we walk towards the door only to start another conversation up.

We finally were on the road after 30 minutes of all that talking inside. It was a nice car ride into the country where their home sat all alone with no one around to bother them. I did not see the wrong in this at first. As always, The Lady got out and immediately went to her room to hide and sleep as she always did. I put my bags down and took in the smell of the living room/. It smelled like peppermint and rain. I enjoy this smell. I do not notice Him watching me as I move around the room, sneaking a piece of chocolate in my mouth then looking at their movies to find out what to watch. I settle on FULL HOUSE because I like that show. I lay down on the couch and start binge watching the whole second season.

I did not think anything of it when He came in the room during the middle of the episode when DJ is at a party with boys, and I hear Him come up to me. He looks at me and smiles and I smile back at Him. Finally, someone is acknowledging I exist. "Don't tell anyone, but you are so beautiful." I just laugh and hug Him, and He returns the favor with a kiss. Something inside my heart just twists and I cannot breathe, but I play it off like I am not bothered even though my privacy has just been violated. This is just the beginning.

I got up to get some food and He comes up behind me and grabbed me from my waist, and we started swaying from side to side. I did not dare to tell Him to stop because I did not want Him to be upset and not want me there anymore. Once again, He whispers, "do not tell anyone honey, but I love you." I turn around and tell Him to stop, that what He is doing makes me feel uncomfortable and He says that He is sorry. He seemed honest and sad about that statement, but I felt relief. He got ready for bed, and I watched Netflix while playing on my handheld.

Occasionally The Lady would come out of her room and make her way to the kitchen to make some food. I would hear her and hide under my blankets because she can be mean. She yells at Him every time He does something a little wrong. I feel bad for Him sometimes when it happens but as a kid, you must leave it alone and let the adults handle the situation when it happens.

I woke up the next day to Him sitting in His chair and he was staring at me. I do not know how long He was staring at me, but I do know it had been quite a while. He stood up and came over to me and gave me a piece of chocolate. The words DON'T TELL ANYONE were basically plastered all over His face and I knew what was going to happen next, but I never said anything. I never said no.

This went on for years, and it got so bad that I missed dinners and would hide in my room to spend my nights in solidarity. I went over to His house so much more than I used to. My family told me I was a completely different person and I hid out more, but in reality, I was trying to find solace in the quiet, trying to find out my purpose for being here, which felt as if I were only here for other people, and not for myself. I swear, I have never felt so lost in my life and I just wanted it to stop but I could not. I used to be just a little bit happy even if no one listened to what I had to say, and I wanted people to love me for me, but I just had this big secret I could not tell anyone.

You see, as a kid, no one believes you over adults, so you are left to deal with it on your own. I do not think a kid should have that responsibility when your parents could easily jump in and help you, but that is just my take on it. No matter how much I wanted it to stop, I could not say no. How could I say no, if that would take everything away from me? I finally had someone I could talk to every day on the phone, for hours upon hours. I could visit Him whenever I wanted to, and it was the quietest place ever despite the growing dread of what would happen when I was there. It was familiar despite the bad, and I could not break that.

CHAPTER FOUR

The day of my 16th birthday rolled around, and He did not have the pleasure of keeping me all to Himself. We had invited some church members to share the celebration with and they spent the day chatting with me, and I could see Him in the distance all quiet. He never came up to me that day. Once He left, I dialed his phone number again and the dial tone was all I heard. I tried again, but with my luck, I heard it again. If He did not want to talk to me He should have at least told me. I do not want to worry about whether I made Him mad. I am mad, however, that He is not answering the phone when I want to speak to Him. Maybe He is busy.

Maybe He went to the store to get some food or things for His horses. Maybe He is working in the shed, or burning some garbage. Maybe He is sitting on His porch watching the birds, or maybe he is working in the barn. Maybe He is watching the phone ring and seeing my name pop up but chooses not to answer.

So I tried calling for days, more than once a day, which turned into months, which turned into me not calling again. I have not touched that phone since then. I did not care anymore, even if my heart felt so heavy, and longed for the connection. I could not dwell on it any longer, however, because I needed to focus on my college and scholarship applications. I pushed my worries to the little spot I had stored for everything bad in my head.

I anticipated my college acceptance letters every day I saw that mail truck. I worked 28 hours every week when I was not working on my schoolwork and I was worried that I was not going to get in any. I started to think about Him and I wondered how He would react to me finally going to college. I could not tell Him and I wanted to.

I went upstairs and did not bother to get ready for the day because I was too eager to find out if I would be going to college. There were no college letters in the mail but there was a package from Aunt Evelyn addressed to me. Aunt Evelyn was my Mom's sister, two years younger. She passed away in a car accident three years ago and it changed our family dynamic drastically. We used to see her every weekend and she was an important member of the family, because she was the only person that knew about my situation. To say I miss her would be an understatement.

I do not understand why I am receiving a package from her or why I am getting it now when she died years ago, but I go sit under my oak tree and open the box. Inside I find seven letters for me. Each letter had a different address on it. One was labeled "open now", "open when you get into college", "open when college seems hard", "open when you graduate", "open when you get a boyfriend", "open when you are sad" and "open when you read all these". Making sure no know was around to eavesdrop, I open the first letter and I started crying.

CHAPTER FIVE

Dear Honey,

    You have been through so much in the past few years, and you are overwhelmed at this point. I understand what you are going through believe it or not, and I can now admit that to you. You do not think anyone would believe you because it is a big situation to handle but know that I believe you. Now, it is ultimately your choice if you tell and you tell, but know that no matter what you will get through this. You will wake up every day with a heaviness in your heart and dread placing your feet on the floor to start your day. You will think of Him anytime you are faced with situations that are even a small reminder of the situation. What you choose is how you respond to it. You choose whether you persevere or you break. If you break that is ok. you will get back up again. If you persevere, that is good too. You will have bad moments and you will have good moments.

    When you are ready to open your next letter, just remember I will be here in your heart, and know I will be by your side in spirit. You are not alone even if it may seem that you are. Even the smallest angels are ones you cannot see very well.

Take care, Honey

CHAPTER SIX

On Thursday afternoon, I saw the acceptance letter sitting on the table. I almost missed it at first but the college logo stood out like a sore thumb. I was so quick to open it, all I could do was stare at the paper, trying to process the bolded words, "We are pleased to inform you...with scholarship...start date." Before reading the rest of the letter, a flashback hit me and I was sitting in His house again.

It was morning and He had just got done with the yard work outside. I was watching an episode where the girls were talking about what their future held for them. "I wonder if I would have a future. A future where I mattered and people listened to what I had to say. I want to help people who feel alone like I do. Do you think I could do it?" He looked at me with a big smile that came across His face. "Honey, you will have a great future. We will be in it together and you will have your college degree. I will see you walk across that stage to get your diploma. You do matter enough to do this"

I always remembered Him encouraging college and He always told me I would make it to this point, but I could not tell Him He was right. He would not answer, anyway. That is when the doubts started to set in. What if I get hard classes and I fail or give up? What If I make zero friends and no one likes me? What if my professors hate me, or what if I cannot live on my own? I definitely cannot do this, but I owe it to myself.

Maybe this was all in my head. Perhaps I am overthinking this and can get through it. I am always doubting myself, but maybe I can do this. I walked downstairs to submit my deposit to the school.

As I was on the computer to confirm my acceptance and review my scholarship information, which was a full ride, I noticed the stack of letters from Aunt Evelyn sitting next to my keyboard. I pick up the next one and tear open its paper. I am going to college.

CHAPTER SEVEN

Dear Honey,

If you are reading this letter you have been accepted into college! I am so happy for you and wish I could be here for you through this time. I know you are being faced with all these feelings that are good and also bad. it is probably not what you want to hear but just know that you cannot grow without some form of struggle. I know you can get through this.

College is going to be tough at first. You might not know much of anyone there, your professors will all be new to you, and your classes might be tough compared to high school. This is not out of the ordinary. It is a normal part of the journey.

You might get through an exam after receiving a low score and think to yourself that you are not meant to be there, but that is a normal process for college. It is okay to make mistakes because making mistakes is how you identify your weaknesses. It is how you take those results and change it for the better that matters.

This is your moment. Your moment to explore and grow into your own person, free to be happy and find your purpose without anyone holding you back. Have fun, go to parties, do not be afraid to ask for help. I am always here in your heart when you need me.

Love,
Aunt Evelyn

CHAPTER EIGHT

The days leading up to college seemed as if it took forever. I received multiple emails about student life on campus including all the clubs I could join, the sororities everyone encouraged the girls to join, and the activities that were scheduled every weekend. I spent my free time scrolling through them all, eager to start but scared I would not fit in. I took a leap of faith even if my heart did not want to. I had my bags packed and tomorrow my dad would drive me five hours away to start a new life, one I knew would change me.

The campus was filled with hundreds of students as my dad pulled up towards the welcome sign by the parking lot. We unpacked everything in my dorm and he drove off, leaving me to fend for myself. I was my own person. The welcome weekend was filled with orientation events and multiple icebreakers as I met new faculty and peer students. I got my laptop, mailroom key, meal card, and my student schedule. Each day presented a new challenge. Remembering where my classrooms were, remembering to ask about difficult topics, and consulting the library when I needed help on assignments.

It seemed to be going well until the middle of the semester when mid-terms commenced. That is when the depression hit. The late-night library visits, the crying in my dorm room until I fell asleep, it was all too much. I kept telling myself I would be able to get through this, but all I thought about when I struggled was calling Him. I just wanted to see Him and talk to Him.

I thought about that all week leading up to my mid-term exam. Once I sat down and the teacher handed out the tests, I stared at the first question, my mind going blank. I attempted the questions as well as I could at the time, walking out of that classroom with my head down. I knew I did not pass. When the grades came back, I stared cooly at the screen, the grade showing me I barely passed. I breathed a sigh of relief but could hear Aunt Evelyn speaking to me, "your struggles are not roadblocks, they are stepping stones. You use them to get to the other side of the journey, not to stop you." That is when I saw the counselor.

I told the school counselor everything. I told her how my uncle touched me when I was 13, how he made me believe he cared about me. I mentioned how I was told that it was a special love and I was not to tell anybody. I also told her how he never answers the phone anymore when I need to talk to him. I never cried so hard that day. She suggested I start journaling to get my thoughts out and stop bottling them inside because it was affecting everything. It wasn't just schoolwork, I had a hard time making friends too. I saw groups sitting together in the dining hall as I sat alone. I saw them talk to each other before class started and they would then hand notes to one another once class started. I felt so alone. I tried to join a few clubs, but every time I went no one spoke to me. I tried to do everything everyone else did instead of being myself. I felt like I was watching a show instead of being a participant.

I signed out of therapy and decided to try writing out my feelings. The words were simple, but not simple to get out, even if they were exactly what I needed. Why was I here? Oh yeah, to be someone to help someone. This was my dream, and no struggle was going to stop me.

CHAPTER NINE

Dear Honey,

By now you are probably asking yourself why you wanted to do this. Why go through all this struggle? Think of the oak tree in your old backyard. It did not start as beautiful and tall, it took years and dedication to weather it into something great. It survived through the harshest storms, all to grow deeper in the ground. It stands now to give you solace in your hardest moments. We are like that in a way. We start as something so small and we learn and grow into better people, constantly helping ourselves to help others. Struggling is a natural part of life, and it is okay to admit you are struggling. I hope you have admitted it.

You are probably struggling with making friends, making good grades, or staying focused on schoolwork amidst stress. We have all been there before. The trick is taking it one step at a time, like walking. You cannot just jump to your destination without taking the steps first.

I know you do not have that tree right now at your school, but you can find alternatives. When you feel stressed, I want you to find a place outside, whether it be a bench, a spot by a pond, a tree in the woods, or even just finding a place to take a walk. I want you to sit and just think of what you are struggling with and the impact it is having. Then think about what you could do to help combat it, even if it seems like you cannot. I am here for you, and there are people who care. I promise you that.

Love,
Evelyn

CHAPTER TEN

The rain fell against the windows of the café as I stirred my coffee straw, creating pictures that did not look like anything spectacular. My notebook was open in front of me but I had not written anything in it since last week. The past few weeks had been a round of small victories and setbacks, and today felt like another climb. I sighed, leaning back on the couch when a voice interrupted my thoughts.

"Mind if I sit here?"

"Hello? Can you hear me?" Confused about whether the voice was talking to me, I looked up to see a girl about my own age, holding a plate with a slice of cake. Her curly brown hair framed a face that seemed gentle, with a nervous-looking smile. "You look lonely over here," she added. I nodded, pointing at the empty seat.

The girls name was Lila, and she was in my Biology class. She sat down and asked what I was writing then asked my name herself. I introduced myself after hesitating a bit. I felt this was a prank. Lila's eyes lit up. "That's such a sweet name. Do you mind if I ask what you're working on?"

I quickly flipped my book over and shook my head. "Just my journal. Honestly, I've been staring at it for half an hour and haven't written a single word."

Lila laughed softly. "Do you want to talk about it? Sometimes it helps to say things out loud. We can go for a walk"

I found myself nodding and in the next ten minutes, we were walking along the sidewalk laughing and talking about the teachers we thought were the worst at giving assignments. After about an hour of hanging out, and me spilling the information about my past, Lila's voice grew quieter as she stopped and looked at me. "There is something I have not told many people. My uncle... he hurt me, in ways I didn't understand until I was older. It's taken me a long time to even say those words out loud."

My heart felt like it stopped. It was like Aunt Evelyn was alive. I took a deep breath before replying, "I know what that feels like. Someone I trusted did the same to me." Lila reached across the table and took my hand. "Then maybe," she said softly, "we can help each other heal." For the first time since starting college, I felt something that I had not felt in years, a bit of happiness.

CHAPTER ELEVEN

To Honey,
You have finally stepped out of your comfort zone. I hope your friend loves you as much as I do. I know you are special and anyone is lucky to have you as a friend. Keep that friendship as long as you can. Do not betray her trust and do not let her betray yours.

You are changing and I hope you see it. You are growing and learning from mistakes to make you a better person. You may not feel It but sometimes feelings do not matter. What makes change change is the fact that it allows being better. You have the choice to make that change.

Sometimes friends will not have the answers you are looking for, and that is okay. That is something that someone else will have for you. You need to seek it yourself. Do not break your friendship for this. Friendship is open for growth and change too.

Friends also have their flaws and struggles too. They are people as well. It is important to share what you are going through with each other and not bottle it up. You guys are there to hold each other up even if you do not have all the answers for one another.

Keep growing Honey, and keep on stepping forward on the path you have set out for you. It is a good one.

Love,
Evelyn

CHAPTER TWELVE

Sophomore and Junior year went by like a breeze. I was now applying to graduate schools for a master's in Psychology to become a Clinical Psychologist and I was better than ever. Lila has been by my side through all these years and we have stayed good friends. We requested to be roommates the following semester after meeting and we spent our nights having pizza parties and movie nights. We kept each other accountable for our schoolwork.

When she dealt with issues from home or heartbreak, she would cry to me and I was there to comfort her through it, something I grew to be good at. I accompanied her to her therapy visits when she asked, and we journaled together when we had a bad day.

We were finally ordering our caps and gowns for graduation, which was coming close to the end of the semester. We scrolled through the internet to find cap design ideas which was a big thing for college graduation. I wanted mine to be bold and tell my story, and she wanted to stand out in the crowd. I cannot believe I made it.

There have been days when I thought for sure I would drop out of school and just live on my own, eating ice cream and watching Netflix alone. Then there were days when I read Aunt Evelyn's letters and they reminded me to keep going. Lila and Evelyn have been a staple in my journey. they encouraged me to tell my story.

Keeping my problems bottled up only made things worse. I was scared and lonely and did not know if I was good enough or smart enough to pass my classes. College was extremely different than high school, anyway. I was encouraged to submit my writing to the writing journal, and I did. I was contacted to share my story if I was willing, and

I hesitated at first. I decided that there was no further harm in doing so and I was desperate for a way out, so I said yes. I spent a Thursday night speaking about my experience with abuse and the effect it has on people, sharing how I overcame it. I helped a lot of people that day and spoke with people who had dealt with the same adversities.

I know we all are taught to obey authority and I was told to listen and never tell, and I always agreed. But now I realize that sometimes you have to say no. I told someone because it was never about Him. I will always tell.

CHAPTER THIRTEEN

As the auditorium grew louder with every new graduate that walked in, my heart started to do that thing where it would flip-flop. I was overwhelmed with excitement and nervousness for today to happen. I had to sit down and breathe. I told Lila I would be back and I found an empty spot by the wall outside the auditorium, 30 minutes before the ceremony was starting. I buried my face in my hands and started to cry. I wished my family was here with me. I looked up after a hand dropped on my shoulder and I saw my mom sitting in front of me, her face full of understanding. "I know, honey. I know what happened and I am so sorry that happened to you. Look at you, all grown up. My baby." I started bawling and hugged her, not wanting to let go. "I did it, mom. I am graduating. Your baby is graduating college."

They started announcing the ceremony so I wiped my tears and went to find my spot and Lila. As I walked towards the waiting area, my mind wandered through the years. That year I lost everything, the year I decided to go to school, the year I started growing. I thought about the moments of doubt that almost drowned me, and the letters from Aunt Evelyn that saved my life. I finally saw Lila a few spots down, and we waved at each other. They were more than friends, but sisters in healing.

I stepped onto the stage once my name was called, shaking with every step. I was not nervous, no, rather too excited. The applause was deafening, and I grabbed onto that diploma with the most determination ever. I made it.

Walking up the steps to grad school was the most accomplished feat I have ever been through. My journey was just beginning, and I was excited to begin this new chapter in my life. I pulled a letter out of my blazer pocket, and it was the last letter from Aunt Evelyn. I open the envelope carefully, read the contents, and proceed to walk confidently into the University, letting the doors of the past close behind me.

CHAPTER FOURTEEN

As I look down at the letter I had written to Him a year ago, I reread the words in a quiet whisper, "I remember the pain you caused me. The suffering I went through all these years have haunted me in a way I cannot describe, but I told someone at 16 and I lived. I told someone in college and thrived. I will never forget what you put me through, but I choose to forgive.

There is no single way to heal, or to help. You can only do what you know how to do and what you feel is the best option. I constantly tell myself I should have done something sooner, or say no, but I was a child, and He was an adult. He should have stopped without someone telling Him to.

Now, still alive at age twenty-three, I am equipped with a heart that is both heavy and that is still growing. Trusting In people to love you is still hard, and wanting to walk away is still my first option, but I know that growth is not just about walking away. Growth is letting people love you but still setting boundaries. I struggle still, and I develop new scars people cannot see, but I choose to not focus on those scars as much as they haunt me. They tell my story and how I got here. They made me who I am.

I find myself sitting under the oak tree in my backyard, similar to the one I used to sit under when I was a kid to seek peace through my books. I feel a quiet sense of freedom. Life is still a giant mess, but it's my life now because I chose to tell someone.

SAY NO

Being a victim of sexual abuse myself, I know that choosing to tell someone is hard.

I also know forgiveness can be hard. You are not obligated to forgive anyone.

You also are not obligated to tell anyone. It is your story to tell, and yours alone.

Do not let anyone convince you otherwise. Do not let them steal your voice

        I promise the strength will come someday.

www.ingramcontent.com/pod-product-compliance
Lightning Source LLC
LaVergne TN
LVHW051926060526
838201LV00062B/4709